the
girl
who
then
feared
to
sleep
&
other
poems

angifi dladla

the
girl
who
then
feared
to
sleep

& other poems

deep south publishing

THE GIRL WHO THEN FEARED TO SLEEP & OTHER POEMS
© 2001 by ANGIFI DLADLA.

DEEP SOUTH PUBLISHING
P.O. BOX 2482, Cape Town, 8000, South Africa.

Grateful acknowledgment is made to the publishers of New Coin, New Contrast and Tribute in which earlier versions of some poems first appeared. In some of them I used my pseudonym – Muntu wa Bachaki.

Production: Robert Berold, ISEA, Grahamstown.
Paul Wessels, Deep South Publishing, Cape Town.

Deep South books are distributed to the trade by
University of Natal Press
Private Bag X01, Scottsville, 3209

ISBN: 0-620-27777-7

Printed and bound by CTP Book Printers, P.O. Box 6060, Parow East, 7501.

Publication of this work was made possible through funding from Buchu Books and the National Arts Council.

NATIONAL ARTS COUNCIL
OF SOUTH AFRICA

contents

exhibits

in this world

dreaming

song of a fertility doll

call me between your tears and eyes;
i'm the shadow, i won't drown.
draw me between your pain and faith;
i'm the shadow that leads.
will me within your heart of hearts;
i'm the energy that's divine.
hug me with the arm of your heart;
i'm reality, i am love . . .
listen to the silence in silence —
the dream materialising . . .

exposure

i heard the back door open.
like a wheelbarrow,
i raised my head
and leaned on my elbows.

someone was inside . . .
the voodoo and the electronic
securities must be in deep sleep
with dogs and neighbourhood watch!

feet and hands paddled,
towing the long body
right into our bedroom
three meters above the floor level.

my stepfather? no, it can't be . . . !
he never knew where i was,
and never cared even before
he died to leave me in peace.

hovering silently in front of the wardrobe
like an alien craft, he turned
his grey head the way a fowl does:
"please, maboi," he cried,

tears drowning that hairy face,
"forgive me, forgive me maboi."
never had i wronged this man,
nor held him grudges.

seemed he caught my thoughts
as he thanked me, and
glided out backwards
like an ocean creature, relieved.

i shivered and rolled myself
with my snoring wife.

when i told her in the morning,
she gawked at me and chuckled:

"poets are dreamers . . ."

the intangible

even today
through the reedy swamp
of katlehong
and vosloorus
as one passes
one will still hear
a lonely voice,
"count me among the dead,
count me among the dead . . ."
sinking like a coffin lower and lower
the further one goes.

even on sundays
as one passes
one can notice
holy men and women
in blue or white
taking rhetoric dives and blobs
in the watery realm
in search of a vocal mirage
which becomes an echo
the nearer they advance.

the stubborn death
(to the grandchildren of this youth)

when you hear your grandfather
scream and plead for death,
do know he hears the unheard —
the screaming flames;
the groaning smoke.
do know he feels the unfelt —
his dancing self
around screams and groans.
do know he sees the unseen —
the wriggling bodies
with bellies distending
into gargantuan black bubbles
which just erupt.
do know he smells the unsmelt —
the charcoal of faeces
protruding like stumpy tails.
do know he was a match —
stick, he was!

confession

one sunday, a hairy man
shuffled and limped
towards our faith healer.
sweethearts of filth and decay
accompanied him,
expressing love.

this might be jesus
trying us . . .

torn, muddy and helpless
as if fished out
from a phlegmslide
of a volcano, he
stretched his feeble arm
crying or praying
for forgiveness:
"i was just a soldier."
his quondam chest
burst into catacombs . . .

dreaming

i thought i was the one dreaming
when voices at the field of monstrous butchery
i heard, with these ears, these ears.

"we are all dead, all finished."
"nonsense!"
"all and — you too, can't you see?"

nothing i saw but the place i knew
had turned into a red swamp.

"shut up!" barked another voice.
"life," retorted the first voice,
"after such frenzied devilry?"

nothing i saw but bloodied shoes and
shreds of flesh on the razor fence.

off to my sangoma i sidled,
fearing the phantasmic voices of dagga
a sister once warned me about,
would hoax me off my head again.
smilingly, my sangoma said i was growing,
and i simply said she was dreaming.

out i went, gingerly of course.
not even a birdsong i heard,
but the voice of my sangoma,
"you are growing, you are growing . . ."

the sacrifice

deception
impression
hiding
morning after hiding
rubbished
portrait of a bully
ubuntu
a voice white as a ghost
fetching
blood drizzles
kazi ngo shona phi
so turned a taxi
vacancy
at the government mortuary
shooting
in the night
exodus
bodies
love
tomorrow

deception

when the thunderbolt scythes heaven
and heaven, in turn, bolts it loud and red-hot,
we salute the spectacle of spectacles —
the inspiration of orators on must in the palanquins.
when all the illusion is over;
the sky remains clear as ever,
so with our heroes up there.
down here — protracted
pain and destruction . . .

impression

off i flinched,
drained
dizzy and dazed.
behind; outsize
black wound
in the earth
where the tyre has nailed him.
human gravy in the sun . . .

hiding

while with an infant in a hide-hole,
far away you hear fanatic thunder
dismissing a duet of owls.

then nearer, nearer, you hear
the steps, intolerant and tempestuous . . .

like a pen-knife
you draw yourself together
and transform into a kangaroo.

then, from that awkward pouch,
the infant yells . . .

morning after hiding

our bedroom
was made of holes and shreds. our bedroom
was made of dust and frozen echoes.
on my pillow a cartridge
lay morose
like a woman after a fuck
that went wrong.
in a nest of pieces,
a grenade . . . brooding.

suspended animation.

rubbished

his body has ended its run,
but his friends are still on the run.
his eyes will never see,
but green flies will lend us theirs.
his lips have lost the power
as his wounds have stolen the thunder.
where his prints have been trampled over,
his corpse remains as a book
— a copy of hell!

portrait of a bully

humping his back
and displaying his fiery grins
of lethal fangs and claws,
this huge brother is god;
our all in all — collars us
all under his sky.
and rubbishes laws of nature.

ubuntu

scattered around
like divining bones,
these smouldering bodies,
smelling like smoked bacon, and
those in puddles of blood —
do not need mediums . . . !

mortals go on with their lives;
paraphernalia of the scatterings.

a voice white as a ghost

you ramokonopi toddlers, triers of catapults and squirt guns on
us
you phola park women, snatchers of our helmets for
chamberpots
you kathorus witchdoctors, cutters of our testicles for
self-sanctification
you katlehong fowls, playing hyenas to the dogs over us
yerrrr . . . who told you we are black meat, who told you, eh?
i am koekemoer, veteran of angola
katlehong peace-maker by day
these are my hardened men, boers of cuito cuanavale
these look-alike black faces we wear, are not for comedy
i know this beastly boy — mabina as a student
not as a terrorist by night — shh . . . !
here comes the commander-in-chief for our remains . . .

fetching

o! eternal one,
mighty spirit of fanabo,
fanabo of the battlefield;
i am maboi, your uncle,
i come with lephoi, your aunt:
   the hour has come;
   the hour has come.

o! formless one,
undying spirit of fanabo,
fanabo of the battlefield.
listen to the talking drum;
the incensed drum of your beautiful clan:
   let's go home, home with the fetch;
   before your divine journey begins.

blood drizzles

blood drizzles under the mattresses
turning the huge room into a swimming pool;
tender and desperate things
float in the red as some little
creatures try to swim
for their lives. they have heard
the thunder and saw the flashes.
underneath the door, blood flows
joining other tributaries . . .

a river rages to the red,
red ocean of the continent.

kazi ngo shona phi
(i wonder where i should go)

like a flea
at the mercy of thumbs,
here i am
between left and right.
the distance is the same
my blood, my soul.
listen to the sputtering of spouts
as thumbs dance a smashing dance
at the festival of blood . . .

so turned a taxi

so turned a taxi
into a lightning-bird
warming up,
but whirled in volumed flames
for failing to fly.

we would later encounter
an unidentified object;
fused iron and bones.

vacancy

red
shoe on the railway
licks shuddering wounds, and
wails like a cheated
coffin.

at the government mortuary

still bodies
white, black,
pinkish and bluish
on one another
like huge matchsticks
in a nude court,
glare at the foul sun
to the amusement
of armed bodies . . .

shooting

face twisted
formed fumaroles;
mouth opened
as if nose blocked;
stench of breath
foreign to the living;
flames of eyes
played a hypnotist.
such is death's pose
for a close-up photo
of my life.

in the night

in the night of shell hell
we hid at the graveyard
to get used to death.
in the night of hell shell
we hid the weak at the morgue
to cool their nerves.
in the night there is a hell
of a way out, there is.

exodus

and i saw . . . all.
all staring with empty eyeballs.
all chewing grass like sleep-walking cattle.
all drooping like beaten finalists.
some with drained babies on their backs,
others with goods wrapped with blankets,
others still dazed from gang-raping
while the pregnant shuffled behind like penguins.
don't look back,
the smoke . . . !

bodies

bodies at the morgue
seem to be waiting
for partners . . .

waiting, waiting still
like nothing

bodies at the morgue
seem to be so
for good . . .

so poor and dull and so
low

bodies today;
nobodies tomorrow.

love

love, listen to hate;
lords of your tribe sing
dogs and birds of prey.
save us, save love and name;
kill me, kill me my love,
kill in one go.

tomorrow

tomorrow, i'll rubbish someone's airspace.
no one will intercept me, tomorrow
i'll get out, out to the . . . worlds
of true gods. there
i'll tell about hunger
in africa, asia, europe, america
and all the islands while someone dumps
tons of tons of fresh food into the vomiting ocean.
i'll tell about the total ban of relevant medication
and technologies to the slums, shacks and the hovels.
i'll tell about people owning more than one palace
while small men live or die in the parks, pavements and holes.
i'll tell about effrontery to the aged
while their epic harvests are in the palaces and granaries.
i'll tell about the jolly fat fellows who barter
our crosses for their show once every four or five years.
i'll tell about war on butchery
while flesh steams on tables.
i'll tell about the real funder
of fires and saws on forests.
i'll tell about the real funder
of lies, germs and genocides.
i'll tell about the real funder
of buriers of souls of great teachers.
i'll tell about the real funder
of lies, germs and genocides.
"oh gods!" i'll cry, "disarm the son of man
before his fear explodes; remind him
of who he really is." tomorrow
i'll fly out of my . . . body.

exhibits

exhibits
from sunrise
peace initiatives
when i was a child
a long riddle
rotting
an intruder
images from mam' yang-chaza's tavern
balloons
remembering zanyana after four decades

exhibits

your horrors
from the beginning of that time
are deeply implanted in us
your crime

whenever we go
people tut-tut and ask
what went wrong

you cry with us
but with one eye
while steadfastly answering in
tomes of stories
tombs of theories
still crime

your teeth and claws
implements of your orgy
grow within us
thin us into raw things

whatever good we
try for ourselves
the famous ones
instant billionaires
up there tut-tut and feel
guilty if there is no pain.

look at us
your casualty
your blackgold

no use to laugh away your shame no use
no use to smile away your heritage no use

we are yours truly
final solution

from sunrise

at the malls,
eastgate, westgate,
northgate, southgate, and
all the gates,
even imposing ones
with glass complexes
caved into mazy bunkers
where escalators show
phantasmagoria — whites
of all ages in all seasons
from sunrise to sunrise
with their apprentices
eat and eat and eat . . .

on the reserves,
hovels, camps,
slums, dumps and
all the burrows,
even the darkest
with dusty cul-de-sacs
where death shows
solidarity — shadows
of all ages in all seasons
from sunrise to sunrise
with their paws
carry blood and
curses . . .

peace initiatives
(midnight·shift)

swift.
nightmare things
pounce here
and melt there
as whirling rays
and crystals.
hi·tech hell of peace . . .

peace initiatives
(midday·shift)

heavenly.
nightmare things
in white feathers
of doves hover
in the sky
like a flock of kites
fanning love
on cords of spiders.
peace capsules of hell . . .

when i was a child

when i was a child,
i hurt and maimed and killed for fun;
i pulled noses and ears of things,
i stoned things,
i hunted things.

when i was a child, i was a whiteman.
high up where danger
snarled, i broke things
even when the winged hovered above
pleading with teary songs, i broke things.

when i was a child,
i unearthed things the way whites do with ancient things;
i stole things the way whites did with something called
                                        kunta kinte,
i snatched from the breasts the way whites did with something
                                        called the aborigines,
i paraded things the way whites did with something called
                                        hottentot venus,
i isolated things the way whites did with something called
                                        red Indians,
i buried things the way whites do with something called
                                        blackman's history.

i was once a whiteman;
but i was afraid of white folks,
they all looked alike — their ways are
all superlatives . . .

a long riddle

seeds in a calabash-rattle,
full of life
yet not for life
as they honour
a self-collision course
without caring
who they are
or where they're from
— remind one
of a herd of cattle
always jostling
against one another
at the dictate
of a whip
(made from their skins)
yet all, in turn, end up
in the slaughter-house
where, in turn, they sing
a tearing capella
— remind one
of the buttocks
always behind
— remind one
of er —, er —, er . . .
guess what
new friend of mine?

rotting

i don't know what missis says today.
can she say something,
today?

i remember her
no-nonsense "i don't-want-flies;
i'm-not-rotting . . ."

with her perfumed fan
always in the mirror
she used to sweep them balletically
away or let me detain them
in the dungeons of my dark hand, or
let me shower them with lethal vapour.

but today in the dust — large
large green flies
in her nostrils like warplanes
on a ghastly mission,
buzz and buzz and buzz . . .

i don't know what flies say to us.
do they say something,
to us?

an intruder
(for illinge high, 9 august 1979)

i didn't see him, i was on duty;
he saw me, he was on duty

swifter than a whirlwind
he greeted me with balls
of fists and yellow of teeth.

i can't say how far, a paper in the storm i was.
i can't imagine such storm, at dreamspeed it went.
i couldn't feel the blows, too fast they were.

boys stormed at him;
the yellow, vacant laughter —
that i saw!

"don't kill him, he's a loony!"
yapped the girls.

i recovered;
i felt the blows:
mad, sharp and hot.

"he's insane, meneer,"
mourned the headmaster
in a tone of oozing laughter.

out i limped,
full of revenge
and shrapnels . . .

images from mam' yang·chaza's tavern

this bottle

it looks innocent
like the fire of the firefly,
this bottle
whose spirit now
plays on the organ.
ah, the spirit,
combustible and so serendipitous,
plays on!

they look statuesque,
these thighs
whose beauty now
entrances the hand.
ah, the hand,
feverish and so irrepressible,
dances!

it looks decorous,
this hand,
whose fingers now
drunk without shame
page the thighs.
ah, the thighs,
suave and so glowing,
dance!

nightlife

there at the tavern,
a display of cars
in all shapes
and hues as if
it's a visit
of a head of state.

there at the tavern,
men and women
of exotic status
and nasal english
relax in prides
as if they are lions.

there at the tavern,
sons of africa
sneak in daughters
of asia and europe
as if it is still
grand apartheid.

there at the tavern,
one will hear:
"onga jayvi uya loya,"
so goes the chant —
if you don't dance,
a witch you are.

there at the tavern,
a girl dances,
as if she's deboned.
her child sucks coke and
rocks laced with whisky
as if it's a veteran.

there at the tavern . . . pretty good!
they are electronics with dance;
they are cyclones with dance,
they are monkeys with dance,
they are snakes with dance,
they are ferns in a breeze with dance.

there at the tavern,
men and women
married with the married,
dance in pairs
a delicate dance

as if they're waves.

there at the tavern,
men and women
guzzle to the point
of hearing witches on the roof;
guzzle to the point
of dancing with tokoloshes.

there at the tavern,
in the spirit of simunye —
they talk in tongues . . .
latin, french, portuguese;
spanish, russian and, fanagalo;
but certainly not in swahili or zulu or amharic.

there at the tavern,
thorough and clear;
on their knees, bellies
and backs — a classic
conquest and humiliation
as if they are africa.

peacock dance
(midnight special)

a song, a circle and claps,
african-style.
a hen, a cock and chorus,
dialogue-style.

graceful, colourful, full,
arrogant, ungettable and cruel dance.
she wears a peahen.
impressive, energetic, toilsome,
sacrificial, suicidal and fan dance.
he wears a peacock.

on she dances, ignoring him, the loser.

hard he dances, stuffing her with paper money.

a song, claps and chants;
fans toss money into the circle.
one by one, they dance around her.
one by one, money remains with her.

the winner sees by flickers — a pink tongue
thinning to the point of a palm leaflet,
widening to the point of her own palm, and
gyrating in three dimensions
while the hands and the waist gesture him to come duze.

ululation, whistles and chants,
african-style.

only a goal scorer knows such ecstasy.

into a proboscis the tongue turns
and locks itself in his mouth.

ululation, whistles and chants,
african-style.

together they dance
as they exit, singing:
mohlang ke nyalang,
ke tla lla jwale ka piano . . .

sheba ka moo
(face this side)

from the tavern, he brings kisses —
fresh offensive of fumy breath
before dawn. for this
a gasmask she wears.

such act he condones; but asks,
as man is all bad breath after all, for all

other parts intact. for this
a woman-sized, masked doll that lolls
takes over.

balloons

balloons, messy as mangoes,
are toys to these cherubic children
in the glittering morning
on the pavement.

mucous hands of pastime,
silvery faces of slime
curse my loving wife
roundly.

little legs of children — needles
of sewing machines,
scuttled . . .

remembering zanyana after four decades

river thaka, as i bring you this offering,
twisted pain i see . . . in your mirror:

in the ancient town of othaka,
a town of ancient birds and flowers,
there lived a woman called zanyana;
a woman, this zanyana, who once cried:
    "o! there rope go . . ."

in all othaka, till to this hour,
no beauty dark and tall as zanyana
whose sole foible was liquor,
liquor foible that made her cry:
    "o! there rope go . . ."

dark were the clouds, bright was zanyana
on secrets and routines of housework.
she then crossed river thaka at noon
for a painful drink that made her cry:
    "o! there rope go . . ."

on all her way, hands would wave:
"lady zet, we greet you, lady zet!"
she would kiss her own hands
and send by air waves of kisses.
    "o! there rope go . . ."

in the ancient township of othaka,
an ancient drink she drank
and sang and argued and joked
with friends or thakians and strangers.
    "o! there rope go . . ."

in all othaka, till to this hour,
no rain cold-blooded as on that day.
"rain or no rain, home is home;

river or no river, home is home."
    "o! there rope go . . ."

river thaka roared, roared
beyond all roars we know —
the whole demon hordes, perhaps
roared to the top of demonic roars.
    "o! there rope go . . ."

one step, "lady zet, no . . . !"
another step, "lady zet, no . . . !"
third step turned zanyana upside
down into a disappearance.
    "o! there rope go . . ."

in the straight intestine of river thaka
a naked, oh a naked torso appeared, "help! heeee . . . !"
along the makeshift margin we ran, we cried and
threw a desperate rope, "hold, o!"
    "o! there rope go . . ."

pythons of brown, brown waves
twisted and swaddled and rolled
her away, as if their right it was.
we scampered, we men of men, scampered.
    "o! there rope go . . ."

in this world

whiteness
blackgold
our bodies
epitaph
the warrior
homecoming
dogs and fowls of radebeville
the dead
the girl who then feared to sleep
how close we are
granny's last lectures
missing
in this world
as you demand
the building, the weapon and the way
song of the aged

whiteness

in the antarctic season of our life
where whiteness is the equation
of eternal terror and obsession,
we question the existence of god.
in the antarctic season of our life
where our heroes evolve into yetis,
we lament africa's waste of labour pains.

blackgold

the energy stored in you in ancient times
does not serve you, not at all;
not even a tree or pot plant that survived.
yet you burn for someone
who does not need you to the future.
your ashes are a paining obituary
of inventiveness and hard work and sacrifice
of shadow-senselessness and stone-passiveness
and womb-darkness that gives light,
beauty and comfort to the world, oh native!

our bodies

our bodies
are practically entrances
and exits
for the open-
ended drama of gore.
even in the grave,
worms, white
as if practically all fat,
loot us dry.

epitaph

here lies ngqulunga, alone
planted like a probationer
in him — the grave secret
that sought light and flowered . . .
may vlakplaas, that horror plant
not creep as vietnam landmines
in our gardens . . .

the warrior
(dedicated to a stone)

free like air, you had been here
willing to free at all costs . . .
eternal like light, you had been here —
the first people chanted your praises;
our children chanted your praises
defying monologues of giant fire.

dust are fires of yesterday,
fossils are goliaths of yesterday;
but not you, you warrior
of the weakened, warrior
of the flattened, warrior!

stone, warrior of all times —
you shall be here,
we will be here
singing for posterity
where we started . . .

homecoming
(for phindile mfethi and mbuyisa makhubo)

you all melted away
like dumb farts.

only the smell
remained . . .

after the abrupt end
of the blizzards,
they all knelt and kissed
the airport soil.

your smell not there,
no one cared.

dogs and fowls of radebeville

whenever my people talk, they do not
talk of dogs and fowls of radebeville.
now i tell, i tell it all to tutu:
in this part of katlehong, dogs
and fowls feasted on human flesh.

whenever my people talk, they do not
talk of dogs and fowls of radebeville.
now i tell, i tell it all to tutu:
in the moon of nyarubuye;
the year of madness in rwanda,
we stormed the laager. and,
then, inventive dogs and fowls
of radebeville waylaid all the drunks.

whenever my people talk, they do not
talk of dogs and fowls of radebeville.
now i tell, i tell it all to tutu:
after the fall of the laager, we
fettered at the freedom square
dogs and fowls of radebeville.
two marksmen; young musicians,
rendered a tune with an ak-47
and a scorpion — we danced
to the tune of shosholoza.
cups and glasses rattled and
rattled and rattled . . .
— a toast of dogs and fowls!

the dead

raggedly brown
and pitifully dry;
the dead, exhumed
for re-burial, are not
a curiosity.
i say this in passing:
our city has a daring collection.
ours hunt, eat, drink and
ask extempore — but the mayor
buries them from visitors.

the girl who then feared to sleep
(for my daughter)

doctors and nurses told her.
she was dying,
the girl who then feared to sleep.
doctors and nurses warned us.
we must fetch the dying,
the girl who then feared to sleep.

she did not fear the sunset,
she did not fear the sunrise,
she did not fear the disease that plundered her,
she did not fear the complications that maddened her,
she did not fear the pains that twisted her —
sleep was what she feared.

we wondered what images exploded in that head.

when sleep stalked towards her,
my girl, dazed, became a spirit dolphin
shooting herself up, recklessly
and rattled her exoskeleton to all the rooms
and made the blackest coffee
and let the cacophony of rattles, bleats, hi-fi and tv sets flare.

we wondered what images exploded in that skull.
we tried to help and purchased help. no, she feared.

when sleep finally ambushed her,
she would talk, groan and chew something
probably scarring off the claws of sleep.
on discovering she had slid into sleep,
my girl, taller than usual, would perform the ritual —
rattling up and down the rooms.

we wondered what images exploded.
we tried to help and purchased help. no, she feared.

one morning in spring,
she was all hope and health.
and all day long
she exuded life and joy
till the sun bled beauty.
then, alone, she heard the steps.

she saw death.

she had no words,
but rattles,
she was all rattles
and jerks!

how close we are

where i come from, i couldn't dance a tango;
where i come from, i couldn't dance indlamu —
        but here girl, even in the toilet i dance.
        neighbours do not see or hear,
        their senses are for birdsong.

where i come from, kids play in the street;
where i come from, kids play in my language —
        but here girl, all in their english bedrooms.
        neighbours do not see or hear,
        their senses are for their own.

where i come from, every child is my child;
where i come from, my sugar is your sugar —
        but here girl, we are our own graves.
        neighbours are not neighbours,
        their smile is their smile.

where i come from, i greet everyone;
where i come from, i visit everyone —
        but here girl, no one talks or waves.
        a neighbour has just moved out;
        black influx lowers the value.

last night at the gallagher estate,
the "who's who" of harambee-masakhane attended —
        i read a poem and shoulder-high was i paraded.
        my short-term neighbour, hysterically, shook my hand
        and trumpeted how close we are.

granny's last lectures

on achievement

child of my child,
alcohol is not for non-achievers —
non-achievers reek with envy, shame and complaint,
they who sleep and fall and sleep on the way,
they with dirt, gobs and stains,
they who survive through lack
of yesterday's records.
coming of age, child of my child,
is not an achievement.

child of my child,
alcohol is for oppenheimer —
oppenheimer, owner of dreams,
carries the universe in the genes;
he, master of visions,
perfects what god had made.
drink today, child of my child,
you have passed matric,
you have found a job.

on devil

child of my child, devil
is not in our tongue;
our tongue rooted in faith
weaves not tales of hate
and vengeance.

evil, child of my child;
springs up from the heart
and head, after within —
the grey head of few words,
loses the debate of madness.

on hell

child of my child,
hell is not hereafter;
but here between
the thighs where even
heroes — wheels in the mud,
dig to be sucked.

hear! echoing a storied-
building, heroes, child
of my child, implode.
but dust, oh child
of my child, explodes
for the world to see . . .

missing
(for matthew goniwe)

naked hand
without a ring
without a watch
tell us, tell
your bare story.

who were you?
which river did you drink?

silent hand
stupefied
mummified
tell now, tell
us all.

who was your chief?
which tongue did you use?

lonely hand
without a voice
without a friend
tell us, tell
your epic.

what brought you
in the paws of law?

shrivelled hand, shrivelled hand
you had been voiceless for so long
talk now, talk your talk
brute hand . . . !

in this world

in this world, dear
life in the womb,
you'll notice cartoon-like smiles
and bedroom eyes
cajole you to sneak
in someone's programme.

you'll feel the intricate smoothness
of diamond and other blessings
romance your hands;
for you for
someone's dream.
can you ignore
such blessings of your lifetime?
the moving comfort
of a swivel-chair;
grandiose tours, and
banquets?
the tickling handshakes,
the hot breaths, and
soft, sucking kisses and,
the media's instant love
for you?
can you, can you ignore
such rituals
of someone's programme?

in this world, dear
life in the womb,
if you're spiritual
you'll see the aura
around such dazzle
betrays mock smiles
and hardware behind
the back.

soon the galaxy —

lips of people's heroes
turn into hairy buttocks
and fart all over your face
unleashing packs of bravoes
and hordes of morons
in your path.
that's when the media
will smear you with polecats'
diarrhoea. doors
will slam your teeth in.

in this world, dear
life in the womb
if you're spiritual,
you'll see heroes
in someone's dream
offer heart, blood and soul
for shots of dews and bubbles of joy.

in this world, dear
life in the womb
history is but someone's dream.
you'll see tawdry history in the screen — the lionized,
even the hour-old,
wear exotic names, and, all
enjoying synthetic ambrosia.

you'll see them
with your own eyes
walking tall on the red;
but always, always
fearing you.
you'll hear them
with your own ears
sloshing on the red
carpet of blood;
but never, never
will you meet them.

in this world, dear

life dare not enter
if you're not an entity
from the gods — peace here
is but someone's flagplants
in our heroes' hearts.

our heroes, oh dear!
are someone's warheads . . .

one day, i foresing, our children's
children and our dogs'
dogs will piss
on shrines and
songs and
images and
smiths and
memorials — or
cinders or
this or
that of critters
of the decaying . . .

as you demand

as you demand this life of mine,
i give these eyes of mine to yours
to glare at you in all your life.
this cry i give, for sure will be
liquid curses within your ears.
this blood i offer will congeal
in your heels and form a pair of hearts
to pump red voices as you walk.

the building, the weapon and the way

the building you occupy, belonged to the enemy;
that's where he wrote tragedies and farces for our people.
his thought forms have formed you into his twin.

the weapon you inherited, carries his impressions.
like a dog used to sodomy, always it will
drive you to inhuman action.

the way you are, is the way he was
growing blindly without shame;
ignoring the rumbling under his feet.

song of the aged

where i used to live, i live no more;
dreams i used to dream, i dream no more,
friends i used to share with are no more,
stars i used to look up to are all gone.

the body i had, is not of today;
the rhythm is all gone,
there is no dance anymore,
I'm a dancer without a dance.

the sun in my eyes is gone;
the smile is dull and cold
like that of a mummy,
I'm a mummy with a heart.

i have lost myself;
my children, my parents, my soulmate, my mates, my
everything . . .
i have lost myself;
my senses, my heart, my mind, my charm, my everything . . .

i've got nothing left now;
only the pension i have,
but noisy vultures — children of my children
without shame swoop upon me.

i've got nothing left now;
oh my man, rubbish me not!
you are there, i'm down
here. our relay.

i've got nothing left now;
but a bright star i hear far, far . . .
within.